To my parents, Carroll and Elizabeth
—L.M.

To Ma
—J.G.

A Just Right Book

Tidy Pig

By Lucinda McQueen and Jeremy Guitar

Random House 🏠 New York

Library of Congress Cataloging-in-Publication Data:
McQueen, Lucinda. Tidy pig. (A Just right book) SUMMARY: A very tidy pig, Florinda spends all her days keeping her house and garden clean and neat until Uncle Werner and his entire family come to live with her and create complete chaos. ISBN: 0-394-80573-9 (trade); 0-394-90573-3 (lib. bdg.) [1. Pigs—Fiction. 2. Cleanliness—Fiction] I. Guitar, Jeremy. II. Title. III. Series: Just right book
(New York, N.Y.) PZ7.M478827Ti 1989 [E] 87-43347

Manufactured in the United States of America 1 2 3 4 5 6 7 8 9 0

JUST RIGHT BOOKS is a trademark of Random House, Inc.

Florinda Pig lived in a little stone cottage next to a lazy stream. She shared her home with a cat named Theodore.

Florinda was a very tidy pig. Every morning she cleaned her house, upstairs and down. She dusted and mopped and scoured and polished. There was not a spot or a speck or a stain left when Florinda was finished.

Every afternoon Florinda tidied her yard, backyard and front. She weeded and mowed and clipped and raked. Florinda even dusted the flower petals of her hollyhocks. There was not a stray leaf or an uncut blade of grass left when Florinda was finished.

In the evening Florinda relaxed by a cozy fire with a cup of
tea and some toast and jam. Theodore napped on the rug
beside her. Together Florinda and Theodore were very happy.

One day there was a loud knock on the front door. Florinda put down her feather duster and went to see who was there. It was her Uncle Werner, who had made millions in the hog feed business.

"Dear Florinda!" exclaimed Uncle Werner. "How wonderful to see you!"

"What a surprise!" cried Florinda. "Won't you come in?"

Uncle Werner, followed by his entire family with all their belongings, bustled inside.

"You remember Cousin Arthur and Meg and their two boys Junior and Mug and my niece Lola and Cousin Wayne," said Uncle Werner.

"How nice to see you," said Florinda. "What brings you to this neighborhood?"

"The swill market has soured," explained Uncle Werner. "The family fortune is lost. We've nowhere to turn!"

"You can stay with me," said Florinda.

Uncle Werner decided to accept Florinda's invitation. Theodore decided to sleep outside.

Florinda's guests soon made themselves at home.

Uncle Werner sank into Florinda's softest easy chair and began to study his books and do his calculations. He was trying to figure out how to make them all rich again.

Arthur and Meg began cookery experiments in the kitchen.

Lola made herself some cinnamon toast and tea and read aloud
from the living room window seat. Cousin Wayne rearranged the
furniture in pleasing patterns. Junior and Mug gathered petunia
bouquets in the backyard.

Florinda picked up after everyone. While Junior and Mug took their baths, Florinda cleaned the kitchen. While the children got ready for bed, Florinda scrubbed the bathroom.

After everyone else was in bed, Florinda dusted the living room.
Uncle Werner was hard at work in Florinda's easy chair. Stacks
of books towered around him. Piles of papers teetered on every
side. Florinda almost dusted his ear by mistake.

The next day Florinda's relatives packed a picnic lunch and went outside to picnic beside the stream. They had a wonderful time eating corn on the cob and watermelon and pie. Cousin Wayne brought out his croquet set and everyone played. Florinda was always one step behind them, fishing corncobs and watermelon rinds out of the stream and plucking croquet balls out of the lettuce beds.

That evening, just as she was scrubbing the last pie plate clean, Junior and Mug came in from the yard with muddy feet. It was half past midnight before Florinda finished mopping the floors. Theodore spent the night in the old oak tree near Florinda's front gate.

The next morning Florinda was too tired to get out of bed. Uncle Werner came up to see her. "Dear Florinda, shall we call for the doctor?" he asked.

Florinda answered faintly, "Oh, no, Uncle Werner. I'm perfectly fine. I just need a little rest."

Uncle Werner was worried. How to cure Florinda?

He went outside and picked
some herbs from the garden.
Then he went into the kitchen
and started to brew an herbal drink.

Some lemon balm for this, some
peppermint for that, a sprig of
sweet woodruff just for good
measure! The possibilities
were endless.

Meanwhile the cousins began to notice a change in the house. Uncle Werner's chair had disappeared. The floor was crunchy in spots and slippery in other places. The furniture was all mixed up. They had to crawl under the bed to reach the pantry. They had to climb over the sofa to get to the bathtub. Arthur and Meg noticed that there were no clean pots and pans. Lola, putting down her book, discovered there were no clean dishes or clothes or bedsheets or anything!

It wasn't long before the cousins put two and two together and realized that they were making a mess of Florinda's house. It was time they tidied up!

They began to dust and mop and scour and polish. They went outside to weed and mow and clip and rake. There was not a spot or a stain or a crumb left in the house when they were finished. There was not a stray leaf or a dusty petal left in the yard when they were done.

Late that afternoon Uncle Werner took his potion up to
Florinda. Everyone tiptoed upstairs after him, anxious to see if
Uncle Werner's medicine would cure her. Florinda took a sip. She
opened one eye, then the other. Something looked different.
Something looked neat. She decided to get out of bed.

When Florinda got downstairs, she could hardly believe her eyes. The furniture was back in place. The floor didn't crunch. She peeked out the window and saw that the grass was cut. And there was Uncle Werner's chair. She'd thought she lost it!

Florinda was delighted. Her little stone cottage was tidy again, inside and out. She started to dance.

Uncle Werner was amazed! The cure he had concocted in the kitchen had worked! Florinda, after just one sip, was dancing! His herbal drink recipe was probably worth millions.

The next morning Uncle Werner and his family packed their
bags and said farewell to Florinda. Uncle Werner was going to go
into the pharmaceutical business! Soon they'd all be rich again.

"Thanks for everything," said Uncle Werner.

"Don't mention it," said Florinda.

She waved as Uncle Werner and Cousin Arthur and Meg and
Junior and Mug and Lola and Cousin Wayne all disappeared down
the lane.

Florinda closed the front gate and turned to go inside. A leaf fell from the old oak tree where Theodore was resting. Florinda ran and caught it before it touched the ground.

All was well!